Slow
Joe

Slow Joe

April Kassel

Illustrated by

Lori Block

Ozark Publications Inc.
P.O.Box 228
Prairie Grove, AR 72753

F
Sar   Kassel, April
      Slow Joe, by April Kassel. Illus. by Lori
Block.
      Ozark Publications, 1996.
      66P. illus.

      Summary: A small girl finds a little opossum in the chicken house stealing eggs. She throws a rock at it. She soon discovers it has only three legs.

      1. Opossums. I. Title.

ISBN Case bound-1-56763-067-7
ISBN Paper back-1-56763-068-5

Ozark Publishing, Inc.
P.O. Box 228
Prairie Grove, AR 72753
Ph: 1-800-321-5671

Printed in the United States of America

Inspired by

the opossum I played with on Grandpa's farm. It had only three legs. Grandpa said, "This little fellow is a boy. I'll bet he tangled with my mowing machine." I named the opossum Slow Joe, because he couldn't keep up with me.

Dedicated to

my grandpa, Dave.

Foreword

A little opossum with only three legs is left behind to fend for himself, because he is too slow to keep up with his family. When a small girl goes to the chicken house to gather the eggs, she finds the young opossum in one of the nests. She picks up a rock and throws it.

Slow
Joe

Grandma Pat went to the

door and called, "April!"

When April ran in the back
door, her grandma handed
her a small basket and said,

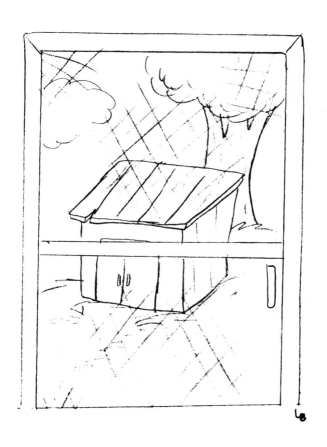

"Please go to the chicken
house and gather the eggs."

April smiled, put the basket on her arm, then skipped

across the field toward the
chicken house.

When she reached the
chicken house she noticed

that the chickens were running away from it.

When she opened the
door and went inside, she saw

something in one of the nests.
It looked like a big rat!

"Get out of that nest!"
April yelled.

The varmint's head slow-
ly turned around and looked
at April.

It was a little opossum,
and it was holding an egg in

its front paws. It paid no
attention to April.

April watched as the little
opossum cracked open the egg

with its sharp teeth. Then, it
turned it up and began eating it.

Again, April yelled at the
little opossum. And just like

the first time, it did no good.
The little opossum kept eating away.

April picked up a small
rock and threw it at the

opossum. It jumped to the
ground and ran for the door.

April noticed that it had
only three legs. She said,

"Wait, little opossum. What
happened to your leg?"

The opossum stopped
running. It turned around and

looked up at April, then said,
"I got it cut off in a mowing
machine."

"Where is your mother?"
April asked.

The opossum lowered its head. "My mother left me," it replied, with a sad look on its face.

April frowned. She didn't
understand. "But why did she
leave you?" she asked.

"She left me behind
because I couldn't keep up
with the others."

April didn't know what
to think. Finally, she asked,
"Where do you live?"

"I don't have a home," he
replied, then added, "I was
hoping to make my home in
the hay barn in the nice, soft,
fluffy hay."

"Grandpa Dave wouldn't
like that," April said. Then,
she asked, "What's your name?"
    "You can call me Slow
Joe," he said. "Everyone else
does."

"Why do they call you
Slow Joe?" she asked.

"Because I can't keep
up," Slow Joe replied.

April smiled and said,
"I'll tell you what Joe, me
and Grandpa are good buddies.
I'll fix things with him so
that you can live in the hay
barn."

So, April helped Slow
Joe dig a tunnel under the
barn wall, and Slow Joe made
his home in the warm hay.

Every day, he made a trip to the chicken house to get an egg or two.

He and April became the
best of friends. And the bond
between them would last
forever.